The Flying Bath

MACMILLAN CHILDREN'S BOOKS

Wings out, and off we fly.
The Flying Bath is in the sky!

Wings out, and off we fly.
The Flying Bath is in the sky!

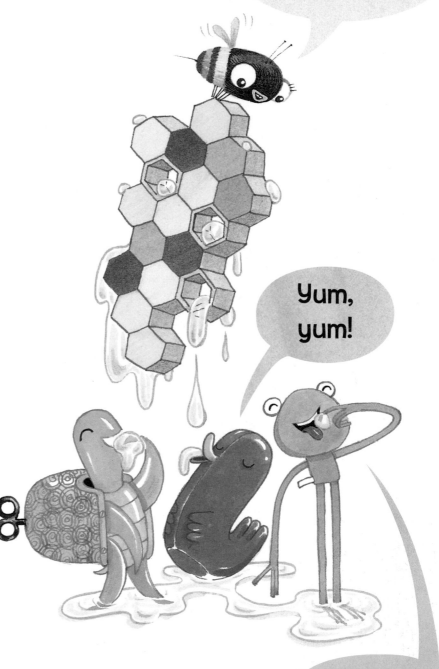

Wings out, and off we fly.
The Flying Bath is in the sky!

Wings out, and off we fly.
The Flying Bath is in the sky!

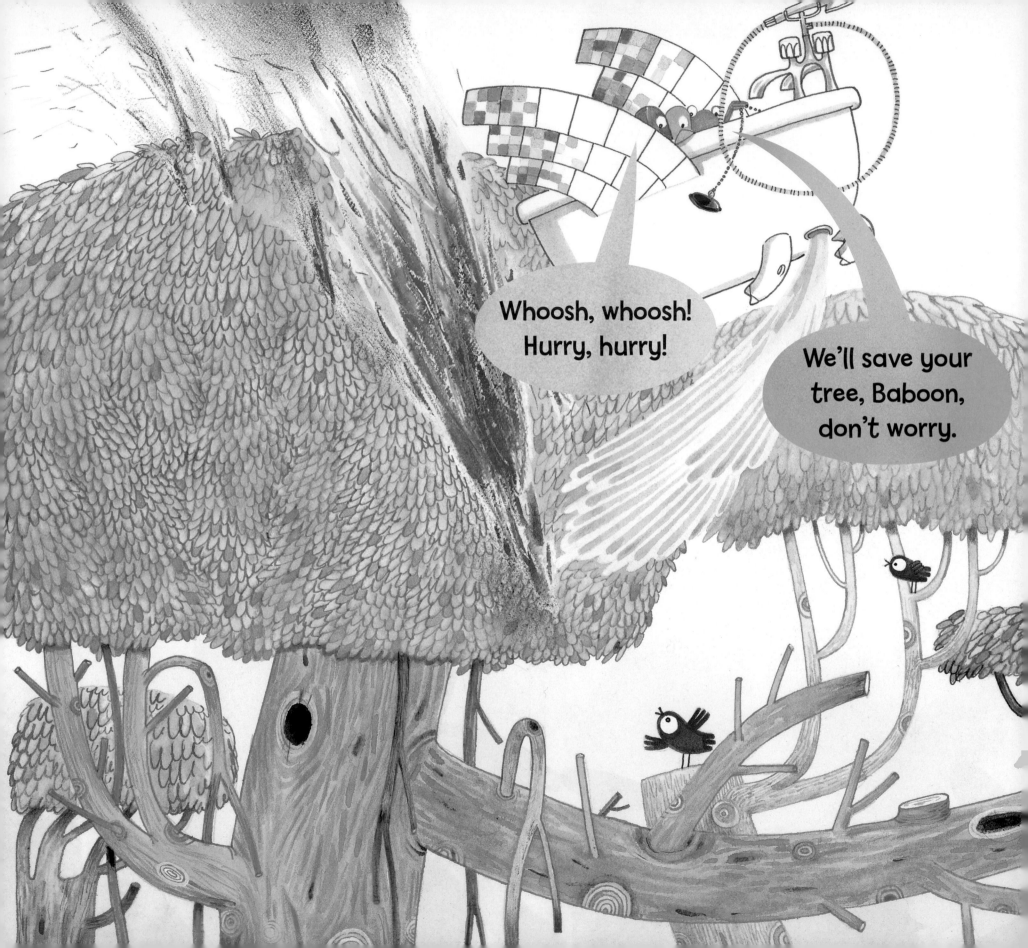

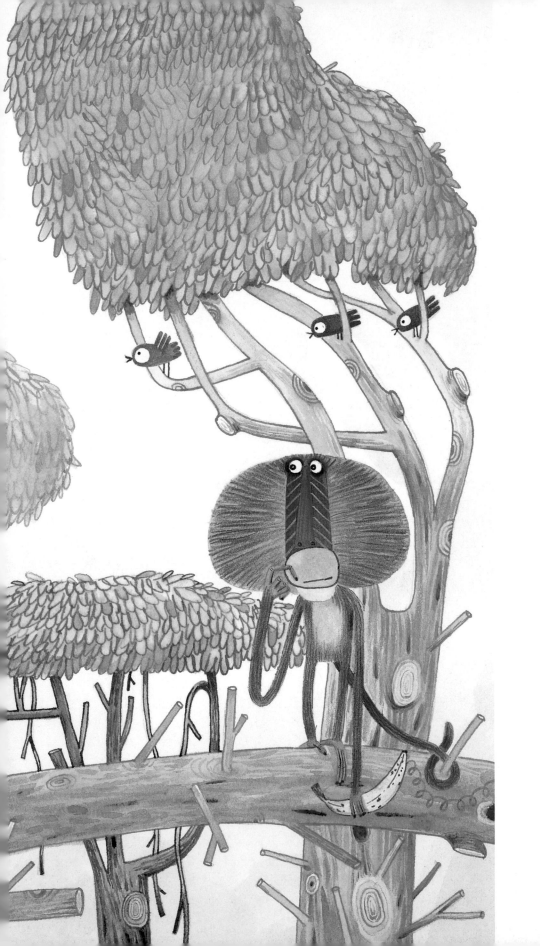

A fish is frantic. There's a drought. He says his pond is drying out.

Wings out, and off we fly.
The Flying Bath is in the sky!

. . . but now it's late.
The Flying Bath has got a date.

Wings out, and off we fly.
The Flying Bath is in the sky!